Barbara

WEEKLY READER
Children's Book Club
Education Center • Columbus 16, Ohio

PRESENTS

JEPTHA

AND THE NEW PEOPLE

by Marguerite Vance

JEPTHA AND THE

by Marguerite Vance

Illustrated by Robert MacLean

E. P. DUTTON & COMPANY, INC.,

NEW PEOPLE

NEW YORK, 1960

WEEKLY READER
Children's Book Club
Edition, 1960

LIBRARY OF CONGRESS CATALOG CARD NUMBER: 60-6008
AMERICAN BOOK-STRATFORD PRESS, INC., NEW YORK

FOR *John Porter*

JEPTHA

AND THE NEW PEOPLE

Chapter 1

AUNT MATTIE dipped her hands into the flour bin, then held them over the sink and dry-washed the sticky biscuit dough from them.

"Now listen to me, Jeptha," she said, trying to sound severe, "you've asked me that question at least twenty times since high tide and I can only give you the same answer: I don't know. So got eat your lunch like a good boy and stop bothering me. They'll get here when they get here; more than that I can't say, so run along."

Jeptha Brewster liked his Aunt Mattie, but he might have downright loved her if she hadn't been so constantly anxious to have him "run along." Father never had, but that day almost three years ago when Father had gone out with old Frank Cooney in his dory and they had not come back—well, that made all the things he used to say and do awfully far away. You tried to reach back to catch and hold so many of them, but

somehow the more time that passed the harder it became. Only Father never did say, "Run along." He
always had time to listen and answer no matter how
often you might ask the same question. Aunt Mattie
might be Father's oldest sister but they were not one
bit alike. That was for sure, Jeptha told himself.

As for Mother, well, gosh, you knew the mothers
of the other boys and girls at school but they were
different. You had only to look at Mother in one of
her pretty summer prints walking down the length of
the *Crow's-Nest* to greet arriving guests to know how
great was the difference. Jeptha once had heard Mrs.
Grünfelder say in the post office, "That Mrs. Brewster's
pretty, maybe, if you like the type. But she's skinny as
an eel and you'd think she could get herself a perm
once in a while, no?"

A "perm" meant a permanent wave Jeptha was almost sure, but what would Mother want with her hair
all frizzed like the black seaweed the tide sometimes
brought in? Her smooth black braids wound around
her head were beautiful, he thought. He liked her
hair that way. As for her being "skinny as an eel," he
had never thought of her as skinny. She didn't bulge
like Mrs. Grünfelder, and on Mondays when the
Crow's-Nest was closed and she wore her yellow
sweater and black slacks and a bright scarf around her
head, Becky, his sister, sometimes mistook her for one

of her classmates in first year high. He liked Mother exactly as she was.

And Mother very, very seldom said, "Run along." Sometimes if it was around lunch or dinner time and people were coming in saying, "Oh, isn't this quaint! How like the Maine I've always dreamed about!" then Mother might say: "Hold it, Captain. I'll be with you a little later." But never "Run along."

Now, walking out into the cool May sunshine, Jeptha thought about the *Crow's-Nest*. He was familiar with the story of how it began: Great-great-grandfather Brewster had opened it as an inn long, long ago; and travelers going north from Portland or south from

Bangor always looked forward to the delicious meals, the open fires and the comfortable beds at the *Crow's-Nest*. With the passing years times changed. Grandfather Brewster closed the inn, keeping only the paneled, low-beamed dining room open to the public.

Jeptha remembered the day only a few years ago when Father, Mother, Becky and he moved up from Plandome to take over the *Crow's-Nest*. That had been when Grandpa died. Grandma and Aunt Mattie stayed on, and to Jeptha it seemed almost too good to be true that at last he was living, not just visiting, at the *Crow's-Nest*. Was it ever fun to fish off the little stone bridge, crabs mostly and sometimes a squirmy eel; and to go out with Frank Cooney when he checked his lobster traps; or to put on your trunks and go tearing down the beach and across the rocks to the water of Penobscot Bay! Even when it was too cold to do more than wiggle your toes in the icy water, just being there was wonderful. Father closed his book shop on Main Street in Plandome, and he and Mother took over the management of the *Crow's-Nest,* the best lobster restaurant on the Maine coast, folks said.

They had all been so happy, Grandma and Aunt Mattie still preparing some of the special dishes themselves while they kept an eye on Katie, the cook, and the three waitresses. Mother, besides being hostess, kept the big brass jugs on the porch filled with flowers from her garden and arranged tiny bouquets for the tables.

And no matter how early you got up, there was Father clipping hedges, hosing off the porch, whitewashing the big rocks that marked off the parking area.

Jeptha had his work, too, even though he had been only six that first summer. He collected all the big white sea shell ash trays and scrubbed them under the pump in the tool shed and then put them around on tables and porch railings again where they would be needed. Becky folded napkins.

Now as he clambered out over the rocks he was thinking about this particular year. It was still early— the *Crow's-Nest* had opened on Mother's Day—and there had not been many customers yet to use the ash trays. He had come upon Mother one morning in hip boots and sweater hosing off the porch. Seeing her doing that seemed strange; that had been Father's job. But she smiled at him as she aimed a stream of water that sent the swinging sign with its picture of a sailing ship's crow's-nest tilting back and forth.

"Hi, Captain Jeptha," she called above the hiss of the water, "how's the boy?"

Well, that was all right, he told himself, but it was all wrong, too. Something, *someone* was missing: Father. Father's not being there to do the morning chores was bad enough, but what really hurt was not having someone to talk to about all sorts of things. The tides, for instance; he could tell you all about those and about who first thought of a bell buoy.

But best of all, he talked with you about horses. No-body around Janesville Beach seemed to care much about horses. Carl Olmstead, back on his farm in Hope, used two big old horses for plowing but nobody thought of them as anything but part of the plow. No one, that is, but Father. He said they were Percherons and once long ago they had been very valuable and were far too old to be working now. One day he had boosted Jeptha up on one and Carl had let him ride it all the way to the barn. Was that ever a day! You got all bumbly inside just thinking about it. But that was the way Father was.

On this particular morning all these matters tum-bled through Jeptha's mind as he picked his way down

across the rocks. He was wearing moccasins because it
was still pretty cold to go barefoot and the smooth gray
gourd-shaped stones were like ice. Three-fourths of the
way down to the shore Jeptha veered to the left where
a shaggy, untrimmed lawn dotted with dwarf-blue
spruce trees ran to the water's edge. The tide was ebb-
ing but water still dripped from the lowest branches
of the trees far out on the spit of land running to meet
the bay. As Jeptha jumped from the rocks to the grass,
water spurted up around his moccasins. He took another hopping jump and landed on firm dry grass bor-
dering a pebbled drive that ran up from the highway.
He stopped.

Aunt Mattie had told him to get his lunch but he

wasn't hungry. Besides, this was the nearest he had
been to the house since the Custers had moved away,
and it seemed a shame to turn back. Any day now the
new people would be coming—the boy would be here.
The boy. . . . Jeptha looked up at the sprawling house
with its long glassed-in porch overlooking the bay, its
field stone pilaster supporting the outside corner of
the porch's roof.

The house had held a fascination for Jeptha as long
as he could remember—even before he came to Janesville Beach to live. When he had come from Plandome
to visit Grandpa and Grandma he had loved to run
over, sure of Mrs. Custer's doughnuts and just as sure
of Captain Custer's invitation to "hark to the shells."
On either side of the mantel over the field stone fire-
place in the Custers' back parlor some enterprising
artist had fastened a large conch shell. Whoever it was
must have been a craftsman of considerable strength,
for the shells were deeply imbedded in the mortar that
held the field stones together and one was faintly
cracked along its delicate outer edge as though the
pressure of the giant fingers had been too much for its
powers of resistance.

One day long ago Captain Custer had said, "Go hark
to what the mermaids in the shells are sayin', sonny."

Jeptha, dribbling powdered sugar from his tightly
clutched doughnut, had stood looking in fascinated
wonder from one to the other.

"Which one?" he asked finally.

"Either one. One's name, this one on this side, is Deborah. Other one's Mary Ann. And they both whisper stories—that is, if you listen close. Now try."

So Jeptha gingerly put his ear close to Mary Ann's dwelling, stopped chewing, held his breath and listened.

Sure enough! From deep within the mysterious pink spirals leading to the innermost recesses of her palace came the soft sighing of—was it wind, or waves rolling up on a distant beach? Or was it a faint voice whispering, "Ah—h—h, Sh—h—h! Ah—h—h, Sh—h—!"?

"Hear it?" Captain Custer pressed a stubby thumb on the tobacco in his pipe and grinned.

Jeptha grinned back and after a minute nodded. "Yes, sir, I do hear *something*. . . ."

"Now, Samuel!" Mrs. Custer came to stand in the doorway and shake a finger at her husband. "You know as well as I do that child could hear the same thing if he'd a mind to hold an empty berry bucket to his ear! You stop putting notions into his head!"

But the Captain winked at Jeptha and Jeptha walked around to listen to Deborah, who gave forth much the same sort of whispering sigh. So a pact was made between them, the Captain, the mermaids, and Jeptha, and after that "harking to the shells" at Captain Custer's house became part of Jeptha's daily routine whenever he was at his grandparents'.

But during the past winter while Jeptha had the measles, the Custers had moved away, to California Mother said. When he was able to be out again the house stood stark and bare, the porch piled high with snow, the map of Maine the Captain had tacked on the sunporch wall looking very lonely as it flaunted its bright colors through the many windows facing the bay.

That had been in January. It was May now and a month since the brief notice had appeared in the weekly paper:

> The former Samuel Custer residence on Route 1, Janesville Beach, has been leased by Miss Beatrice Pomeroy of New York and London. Miss Pomeroy, who expects to make it a summer home, will take possession in mid-May.

Just where Jeptha had heard about the boy he was not sure. Probably at the post office or possibly at school. Somewhere someone had said, "Know the Custer house at Janesville Beach? Well, there's a boy coming to live there." That was all. Now it was "mid-May" and Miss Beatrice Pomeroy and the boy should be arriving.

Wonder what his name is, Jeptha mused, automatically climbing the steps to the outside porch. He almost expected to catch a flash of Mrs. Custer's white apron, a whiff of the Captain's pipe. His name'll be Lennie, I betcha, or maybe Charlie or Fred or Harry.

He pressed his face against a window, squinting, cupping his hands around his eyes. Empty. The back parlor all spread out on the other side of the window, with Deborah's and Mary Ann's houses shining white and lonely in the sunny emptiness.

"Gosh!" Jeptha spoke aloud, the exclamation jarred from him by the tremendous sigh that came tearing up from the very depths of his being. He had not known he could feel this way about an empty house. He discovered that he could look straight through it, across the big square dining room to the north windows and the budding apple trees beyond. When the boy came he must see the thrush's nest, not get very close to it, but just see it, and the trunk of the apple tree where a fox had nibbled a place that looked like the letter "M."

The boy—Jeptha started. A huge yellow van with the words "Interstate Moving Company" on its side was turning in the driveway. Jeptha wasn't sure whether to stay where he was or to slip quietly off the porch at the rear, circle the planting of arbor vitae behind it and disappear. One of the men on the van decided for him.

"Hey, kid, you know who might have a key to this place?" he asked. He and his companion sitting up in the big glassed-in cab looked friendly enough, but the question was so unexpected that Jeptha found it hard to swallow.

"N-n-no, sir, unless it would be the Custers and they're in California. Or—or maybe the post office might know someone. Only both Frank and Hattie Pringle have gone to lunch I guess . . . if it's after eleven. The post office won't be open 'til twelve." He came slowly down from the porch and leaned against the huge front wheel of the van, looking up at the two men.

The one who had addressed him pushed his cap far back on his head and smiled. "Well," he said, "that being the case, I guess we might as well sit and wait for the menagerie to get here. I just thought somebody—some neighbor—might have an extra key and we could start unloading. But looks now as if we might as well have lunch first. Know of a lunch counter around here?"

"Yes, sir. My mother's restaurant 'cross the road, the *Crow's-Nest*." (Boy, is this exciting! The new people's movers coming for lunch!) "If you come now you won't have to wait because it's early. Around one it gets crowded."

The man's companion stopped mid-way in the act of lighting his pipe and peered down at Jeptha. "*Crow's-Nest*, you say, sonny? The dressy shore dinner place? Yep, by George, there it is!" As he spoke he turned slowly and surveyed the *Crow's-Nest* as Jeptha had described it, " 'cross the road." "No, no, that's not for us. We. . . ."

But his friend interrupted. "Why not, Charlie? We leave our caps here in the van, see? Our shirts are clean, so we put on our coats and ties and mosey over just like the union boss at a clam bake, see? Right?" He turned to direct his last question to Jeptha.

"Right! I'll go tell Mother!" Jeptha started off, then skidded to a stop and whirled around. "Are the new people coming today?" he called.

Both men laughed as though they were enjoying a secret joke and the one named Charlie nodded. "Yep, they should be here this afternoon some time. We passed 'em in Portland, them and their Indians and their tiger and their parrot. Wow!" He slapped his friend on the back. "Some outfit, eh, Frank?"

"Tiger? Parrot? Indians?" Jeptha's eyes were shining. "They have a real live tiger?"

Frank shook his head. "Charlie's kidding. They're just a queer bunch is all. Now you were going to tell your mother to dish up or something?"

Jeptha was off across the lawn, across the highway, and around to the kitchen door of the *Crow's-Nest* before his new friends had fastened their ties.

"Aunt Mattie, Aunt Mattie, they're coming for lunch!" He slid to a stop beside the electric range where Aunt Mattie was pouring melted butter for lobster into tiny copper bowls.

"Coming for lunch? Who's coming for lunch? Be careful, dear, don't bounce so! Who's . . . ?"

"The new people! They're here! Well, I mean the movers are, and they're coming right over! I told them to come early because. . . ."

"*The movers? Here?* Jeptha Brewster, you and those new people, whoever they are, are going to drive us all crazy! Today, our first big day of the season, with the Plandome Garden Club having its opening luncheon here, and you must recommend the dining room to a couple of strange moving men! I declare, Jeptha, there are times!" She put down her kettle of hot butter to go to the swinging door opening into the dining room.

The dining room was empty except for Mrs. Brewster who was arranging a bowl of lilacs on a large center table. At that moment the outside door swung open to admit two burly giants who looked about them a little uncertainly then approached Mrs. Brewster. Aunt Mattie backed into the kitchen, colliding with Jeptha as she did.

"Ayah," she sighed, "your friends are here—not a bad looking lot I admit—but you stay out in this kitchen, hear me? You know you're not permitted in there!"

"I'll see the people when they come, though. Charlie and Frank—they're my friends—said they'd be here this afternoon."

Chapter 2

BUT JEPTHA did not see the arrival of the newcomers after all. He had forgotten that he was to be at the dentist's in Plandome at two o'clock and at the barber's for a haircut at three. Janesville was eight miles from Plandome and it was Hattie Pringle, the postmistress's afternoon off, and she had very kindly consented to drive Jeptha both ways. Also, she had errands of her own in Plandome, so it was close to five o'clock when they returned.

Jeptha peered eagerly in the direction of the Custer house and could not believe what he saw. The van with Frank and Charlie aboard had vanished and had been replaced in the driveway by a station wagon and behind it a long, low convertible. As for the house, the blinds were drawn, the door closed.

The following day was Sunday, so school was no obstacle for another twenty-four hours. Sundays were always very busy days at the *Crow's-Nest,* and Jeptha knew that, once his chores were done, he would not be missed. By eight o'clock he was plodding up the driveway leading to the side door of the house which mysteriously was no longer the Custers'.

Because his moccasins were soft he came upon the boy silently, unexpectedly, as he lay curled on the sloping cellar door, jabbing his knife again and again into the pulpy grain of the wood. Jeptha stood watching him for a moment, his breath coming fast. Here, at last, was the boy! This rather slender lad of about his own age—ten—wearing khaki shorts and shirt and woolen knee-length socks above handsome heavy shoes was not at all what he had expected. His abundant hair was dark and curly and longer than Jeptha was accustomed to seeing boys wear their hair. In contrast his own almost white crew-cut hair made him feel suddenly bald.

He wasn't quite sure why, but the boy in some strange way made him think of the picture of the Prince in his copy of *The Prince and the Pauper*.

How did you begin? He gathered himself until his stomach seemed to have turned to a hard rock, then without meaning to, really, he shouted, "Hi!"

The boy jumped to his feet and whirled around, dropping his knife, glaring.

"You—you scared me!" he said. "Who are you?"

"Name's Jeptha Brewster. I live across the road. I didn't set out to scare you. What's your name?"

The boy continued to stare and finally brought out slowly, distinctly, "John Argyle Varick Tewksbury Pomeroy Third."

Jeptha felt strangely defeated. This did not sound so much like a name as it did like the first line of a poem they might be reading at school, something to rhyme with "bird" or "heard" or "curd."

"Pomeroy third?" he repeated solemnly.

The other boy filled in . . . "John Argyle Varick Tewksbury. . . ."

"Ayah, John Argyle Varick Tewksbury Third. It's a lot, isn't it? Do you have two brothers, first and second Pomeroys?"

John drew himself up, looking more than ever like the Prince. "Now, I say, you're being rude," he accused. "No, of course I haven't two brothers. I haven't one. I have Auntie Bee and Salah and Roshani and Amah and Maghra and. . . ."

"Darling! Darling, come kiss Auntie Bee!" shrilled a high falsetto voice from somewhere indoors.

It was Jeptha's turn to jump. "Gosh! Is that your aunt?" The words were a hoarse whisper. "I'll be going. . . ." He began backing down the driveway, but John stopped him.

"Come, don't be an ass! That's only Kirby!"

"Kirby?" Jeptha had been called rude and now he was being called an ass. The combination not only sounded peculiar but it did not set well. "Who's

Kirby? And I'm not an ass and I'm not rude because I haven't got ringworms. Rudie Betsford's rude. My mother said so, and he's got ringworms and I haven't. So quit calling names!"

For the first time a smile broke over John's face. "Old Kirby's Auntie Bee's parrot. I didn't mean to call you an ass. I wouldn't be that cheeky. I just said don't *be* one."

Jeptha found his own mouth spreading in a grin. "Don't your mother and father live here, too? All those people with funny names—are they your aunts and uncles like your Auntie Bee?"

John had slumped down again and resumed his knife work on the door. Jeptha casually twirled the Coast Guard whistle he had found the week before. He had a knife, too, but the whistle would do for today to establish him as an equal.

"No," John answered, jabbing at a particularly hard knot in the wood. "Mummy died when Dad's car was struck by another car when I was a little chap—long ago it was. Dad got his chest bashed in and has to live in the western part of America, in Arizona. I'm going there to live with him pretty soon. . . ."

"You are? For keeps, not just to visit?"

John nodded. "Hmhm, for keeps. He's wonderful, my dad is. Wait, here's his picture." He reached into his shirt pocket and drew out a small leather case which he opened and passed to Jeptha. Jeptha saw a handsome, bronzed man wearing a sombrero, his shirt open at the throat, smiling at him across the saddle of a spotted pony. Here was a man who would never tell a boy to run along, a man who reminded him a little of Father.

"Gee, I bet you wish you were out there right now, don't you? I like your father a lot." He spoke softly. There was no doubting the enthusiasm in Jeptha's beaming expression or the timbre of his voice as he handed back the picture.

John tucked it into his pocket with a happy sigh. "It's going to be ripping being with him," he agreed, "and I'd be out there now except that Auntie Bee opens in San Francisco in September and. . . ."

"Opens—what?" Jeptha was not sure he had heard what he thought he had.

"Her play, of course. I say, didn't you know Auntie Bee is an actress, a very famous one, too?"

Jeptha shook his head.

"Yes, that's how we happen to have Kirby and Maghra and the—the rest. We were in India for three years. That was right after I went to live with Auntie Bee, and she was in India soaking up—I believe that's what she called it—soaking up stuff for the play she was writing then. She was going to produce it, too; then quite suddenly Mr. Blau—he's her manager—told her to come back to London to play in *Says Who,* so we all packed up and went to London again for the whole winter."

"But how come you're here now?" Jeptha found he was having trouble taking this all in: India—London—Mr. Blau—Roshani—Salah—San Francisco. These new people were proving more than he had bargained for.

"Well, Auntie Bee wanted to spend the summer by the New England seashore to soak up some more atmosphere, that was it, atmosphere, for the play she'll open in in San Francisco. She was bringing me home to the States anyway, but there's no New England seashore near Arizona, and Dad's busy building the addition on the ranch house for me when I get there so he couldn't come here just now. So Auntie Bee took this place because it's right by the New England seashore and. . . ."

"Ring down the curtain! Ring down the curtain!" Kirby screamed from somewhere.

". . . and she thought I could learn to swim. Only I don't want to. I'd rather go to Arizona."

"It's too cold to swim here 'til July," Jeptha said, "but maybe you'd like to go fishing?"

But the other boy shook his head. "No, I'd rather not, thank you. I—I don't like water much—I mean deep water."

"You mean you're scared?" Here was something Jeptha could not believe. How anyone could be afraid of sea water was something beyond his understanding;

but there was an interruption, so for the time being he must wait for his answer.

A pretty, smiling, olive-skinned woman appeared at the kitchen window. Great hoops of gold or brass swung from her ears and her head was partially covered with what seemed to be part of her dress.

"Master John," she spoke in a soft voice, "memsahib says you have your breakfast now, please. Salah and Roshani very busy, make order in house. Master John come eat with Amah now, please?"

John jumped to his feet. "I say," he invited, "be a good chap and come and have breakfast with me, what?"

Jeptha had had his breakfast hours earlier and the thought of another did not in the least bother him. So he trotted up the steps with John and into Mrs. Custer's familiar, sunny kitchen. Only it wasn't Mrs. Custer's any longer, he reminded himself uncomfortably. A glimpse into the back parlor showed packing boxes and furniture piled everywhere, with the dwellings of Deborah and Mary Ann blocked from view. A man and a woman, both dark skinned, the man turbaned, moved about silently, swiftly, talking in whispers. Jeptha found himself walking on tiptoe, but John shook his head.

"Auntie Bee can't hear us back here in the kitchen, can she, Amah?" He addressed the woman who was putting blue bowls of cereal on the table.

"No, Master John. Memsahib hear nothing in her big room upstairs 'way in front." She smiled down at John, then to Jeptha, "Come, young master, sit here."

Jeptha slid onto a chair and suddenly some movement in the far corner of the kitchen made him turn to face Kirby swinging his green and red body upside down in his cage, chuckling softly as he did.

"Hello, darling," he chortled. "God save the Queen!" Jeptha laughed until his face was crimson and John laughed with him. Quite without knowing how it happened the two boys were friends.

"I say, isn't old Kirby the silly old clown?" John laughed, busily spooning up cereal.

Jeptha nodded, then asked soberly, "Look, why do you always say 'I say' and then say it? Sounds funny."

The other boy looked at him for a long moment, then he shrugged. "I don't know. Why do you say 'Ayah' when you mean 'yes' or even when you don't mean anything in particular?"

Jeptha knew his face grew very warm but somehow he was not hurt or angry. In his heart he knew he never would be hurt by or angry with John Argyle Varick Tewksbury Pomeroy Third.

The week that followed was the most exciting Jeptha ever had known. There were certain spots in it that he knew he never would forget. There was the afternoon, for instance, when Rudie Betsford and his pal, Cy Brooks, left the school bus with Jeptha just as

John came running up. It had rained in the morning and John had leapt in wide circles to avoid puddles.

"I say," he shouted as Jeptha jumped from the bus, "Auntie Bee says she'll give us tea on the veranda if you can come. She wants to meet you and I think it'll be jolly, don't you?"

His cheeks were flushed, his eyes were shining with excitement. His new friend was here, this tanned, stocky boy with his crew-cut and his funny speech. John loved him. He was the first American boy he had met and somehow knowing him made John proud that he was an American, too. It was being like Dad. Auntie Bee, though she was Dad's sister, might have been either French or English, but not American. Well, here was Jeptha and they could go back into the garden and see the croquet wickets Salah had set up, and after tea he'd teach Jeptha the game. Next week when Jeptha's school was out they could have a real match the way the boys at St. Martin's School in London had.

He was thinking of all this as he ran to meet the bus. Now, breathless, shouting his invitation, he halted, panting, beside Jeptha. A ball of mud struck him squarely in the chest as Rudie Betsford yelled:

"Aah, listen to Jeptha's la-de-da friend! 'I say, let's have tea on the veranda!'" He had scooped up the handful of mud and let fly with it and now he was uncertain whether or not to send another one after it.

For a second John and Jeptha stood, stunned by
the assault. John mechanically picked mud off his shirt
and face; Jeptha found himself numb with a sense
of outrage which he did not quite know how to handle. Rudie and Cy were in his class at school though
both were a year or two older than he. They were a
scrubby pair and Jeptha always had been secretly
afraid of them. Now, seeing Cy's sneering grin as he
stooped to scoop up some mud of his own, and Rudie's
satisfied leer, something in the profoundest depths of
his being snapped.

He was not sure just what made his right arm shoot
out as it did or how his fist made such lightning con-
tact with Rudie's nose. It all happened in seconds,
and then he was down, with both Rudie and Cy
pounding, kicking, gouging from every direction. But
only for seconds. Head down like an angry bull, John
charged into the fight, fists flying.

Cy screamed, "Lemme alone, ya crazy sissy! Quit
punchin' where my sore tooth is! That ain't fair!"

Rudie, dodging the lefts and rights Jeptha was aim-
ing at his nose, flailed his arms about, bawling, "Get
off my chest, will ya? We was only foolin'! Stop hit-
tin' or I'll tell your mother!"

Jeptha wiped blood from his chin and began breathing more slowly. Now I'll catch his old ringworm, he
thought with fury and struggled to his feet. But in
the midst of the fray came Frank Pringle from the

post office and Mr. Blodgett who owned the antique shop, running, puffing, splashing geysers of rain water as they came.

"Hey, you kids, cut it out! Look at you! What you tryin' to do—kill each other?" Frank yanked Cy up by the collar and jerked Jeptha around to face him.

Mr. Blodgett spoke to John. "What happened, son? And you, Rudie, how come you're fighting with boys half your size?"

The stories were quickly told. Voices squeaked to ear-splitting shrillness; a crowd gathered; Bob Peters, the sheriff, patiently laid aside his brush—he was painting his skiff down on the beach—and sauntered over to see what the trouble was about.

"Hmf! Jeptha Brewster, I'll have to see your mother 'bout this, I'm afraid. Ayah, can't have you makin' a fuss like this. Never have before, have you?" He looked down at Jeptha's blood-smeared, dirty, round face and suppressed a smile.

"N-no, sir, but Rudie threw mud at my friend and called him a la-de-da and . . ."

"Your friend? This young feller?" He turned to John. "Oh, you Rudie and Cy, stop edgin' away and stay right here. I ain't through with you. Now then, what's your name? You're a newcomer, ayah, that you are. . . ."

John, busy examining his battered knuckle where it had met Cy's sore tooth, answered as he had answered

Jeptha only a few days earlier, "John Argyle Varick Tewksbury Pomeroy Third."

There was a long silence. The sheriff seemed to be having trouble with his throat. Then, "Oh, I see, you just moved into the Custer place, didn't you? Like it around here?"

"Oh, yes sir, very much." John decided he liked this gentleman, too. Another American. "Could you— my Auntie Bee has invited Jeptha to tea. Couldn't you come, sir? Roshani has made a spice cake. . . ."

"Well, now then, thank you, Pom—what is it?"

"John Argyle Varick Tewksbury Pomeroy Third."

". . . John, some other time. You thank your aunt for me and say I'll be honored to come. But now you and Jeptha go and get yourselves cleaned up. As for you two, Rudie and Cy, I'm giving you this one last warning. If I catch you just once more picking on boys half your size, or on *any* boys for that matter, or pilfering in the store or the boat sheds or abusing animals, I'll take you in and send you upstate where you don't want to go. Now, remember. Get along now, and if you want to send your fathers to see me tonight after chores, that 'd be just fine."

He waved them off and hurried to catch up with Frank and Mr. Blodgett; and Jeptha felt fairly sure he would not find it necessary to tell his mother after all.

He and John went around to the back door of the *Crow's-Nest* to scrub before their battle scars should

betray them. He always loved to think about that afternoon and he rather suspected John did, too.

And it was during the first week—actually, it was
late that same afternoon—that he met Auntie Bee and
Maghra, also something to remember forever. Shining and damply clean, if somewhat bedraggled as to
clothes, the two boys presented themselves on the veranda just as Roshani was spreading the white cloth
on the reed table and Salah was bringing out the big
brass tray of tea things.

Jeptha, on the edge of his chair, wondered what
"tea" would be like. Milk and cocoa were the only
beverages he knew, with now and then a cup of sassa-
fras and fennel tea. These tea leaves came from a little box in Grandma's bureau drawer and the brew
made his eyes water just to think about. "But tea,"
the sort of "tea" the girls meant when they talked
about a "tea party"—this would be different.

He was staring at the screen door opening into Mrs.
Custer's back parlor. He was just about to tell John
of Deborah and Mary Ann, when suddenly a vision
came to stand in the doorway, golden, smiling, and
one could only wonder how such a vision could be
called by the quite everyday name of Auntie Bee.

She's all gold, he thought, letting his eyes travel
from her mop of short, golden curls, across the soft
butter-yellow pullover and the full yellow skirt bil-

lowing about her. She's gold and she looks like a
Christmas doll in the Bon-Ton window!

At that moment the Christmas doll smiled at them
through the screen door and said, "Now this is really
delightful having two such charming young gentlemen join me at tea. And this must be Jeptha I've
heard so much about. How do you do, Jeptha? I'm not
coming out to greet you before I've told you a little
about another member of our family. Maghra is really
a darling. Don't be afraid of her. She's really a great
lady and gentle as a lamb. Up, Maghra!"

Not until then had Jeptha noticed a light chain on
Auntie Bee's wrist, but his heart lurched and he felt
the tip of his nose turn icy as terror gripped him.
Auntie Bee pushed open the screen door and stepped
out on the veranda leading. . . .

"It's a leopard!" Jeptha whispered. He had turned
ashen, his hands gripped the rattan chair in which he
was sitting until the whole chair squeaked. "It's a leopard!" he whispered again.

"No, dear, Maghra's a cheetah. See," as the big tawny
cat padded across the porch toward him, "she wants
to be friends. Put your hand on her head. She won't
bite—really." She came to stand beside him and put
her own hand on the broad head that was bumping
Jeptha's knee.

"Go on, do. She'll love to have you pet her," John
encouraged. So, gingerly, Jeptha laid his hand be-

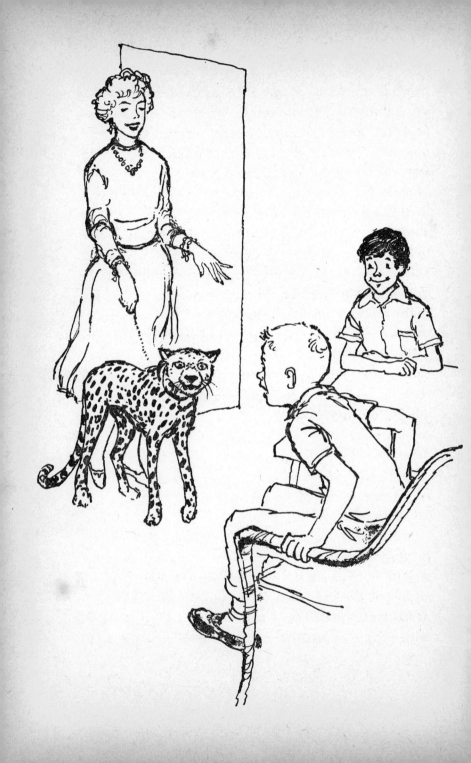

tween Maghra's short pointed ears. Golden eyes looked
up at him and a great rumble which was a purr came
up from the broad chest. Jeptha found himself smiling with pleasure. This big wild animal liked him!
Boy, would it be wonderful to own one like her!
Maghra knew she was making a fine impression on
their guest and began nuzzling Jeptha's collar and suddenly in a burst of friendliness, slapped an emery
board tongue across his chin. This was too much.
With a chuckle of delight Jeptha put his arms around
the big cat's neck and not until Auntie Bee said laugh-
ingly, "That's enough, Maghra, let Jeptha have his
tea now," did the animal slump to the floor.

Tea. So this was "tea," this cup brimming with
warm cream ever so faintly flavored with tea. Roshani
set a little table beside him, passed big slices of bread
and butter and squares of warm spice cake and went
for more hot water. Much as he loved the spicy cake,
Jeptha would much rather have been left alone with
Maghra who was now rubbing her jaw along the side
of his shoe as though trying to prove to him just what
great friends they were.

Still wondering whether this was not all a dream,
he ate his bread and butter trying to believe this mys-
tery of which he was a part. He, Jeptha Brewster, was
sitting on Captain Custer's porch with a live cheetah
at his feet, eating bread and butter and drinking tea
with people he hardly knew but liked very much, in-

deed. He never had known people like them, people who had cheetahs for pets and hired girls with names like Roshani and Amah and hired men named Salah. Perhaps he would speak to John about it when they began playing croquet. But he was beginning to be uneasy; he should be going home. Becky sometimes forgot the napkins or the menus which must be changed from "Luncheon" to "Dinner." He was about to get up when Auntie Bee, pouring herself yet another cup of black tea, turned to him and asked:

"Have you lived here all your life, Jeptha?"

He swallowed a rather generous mouthful of cake. "Yes ma'am. My father, too. Grandma says there's been Brewsters in these parts going on two hundred years, ayah, two hundred." Nodding to emphasize the fact, "My mother," he added, warming to his subject, "she's from other parts—Chicago, Illinois."

"And John tells me you help your mother in the restaurant. That seems quite a job for a boy your age I should say."

"Well, no ma'am. Beck, she's my sister, she helps some, too. Grandma and Aunt Mattie do the most, only Aunt Mattie, she—" he flushed for he knew he had ventured too far, but he stumbled on, "well, she has a boy friend, Caleb Snow, and Grandma says if she up and marries Caleb and goes to his farm up Northport way, we'll have to find us somebody else to help. Only nobody can make strawberry shortcake like Aunt Mattie. The customers all say so."

Where does this solemn, square-rigged boy get his old-fashioned lingo, Beatrice Pomeroy wondered and tried not to smile. If he were in a play he'd bring down the house. Aloud she said, "Well, for all your sakes I hope your Aunt Mattie will not be in too great a hurry to go off to Northport. Still, one mustn't worry about uncertainties, must one? They have a way of straightening themselves out. And before I forget it, both of you boys please remember not to let Maghra off the porch unless Salah is with her. And watch the screen door leading to the outer porch. If it isn't hooked Maghra can open it with one swipe of her paw. If she ever got out alone there is no telling what might happen."

"Would she hurt someone?" Jeptha wanted to know, still feeling brave to be fearlessly rubbing Maghra's chin with his toe.

"No, poor lamb. She would not hurt anyone but herself most likely. She would become bewildered and run blindly, probably straight out onto the highway, and be struck by a motor car. And another thing, Jeptha, you see cheetahs are hunters. They kill sheep and lambs and other animals. So Maghra might run into a field and do great damage. We must remember that. Some day soon Salah will tie her to the back of the car and take her for a run in the country as he used to in England. It will keep her legs and paws in good condition."

In the house the telephone rang and after a moment Roshani spoke from the doorway. "New York calling, please, memsahib."

Auntie Bee disappeared inside with Maghra padding beside her. "You boys go down and try the croquet set now," she called over her shoulder. "I'll join you in a moment."

Jeptha knew he *must* go. He must be wanted at home. Suddenly anxious, he thanked John for the tea, knowing he should have waited and thanked Auntie Bee, and went streaking off across the road. What a day it had been! In his ten years he had not known so much excitement.

"You dreamed it, baby," Becky teased a little enviously. "You know John's Auntie Bee isn't *the* Beatrice Pomeroy. What would a famous actress be doing here in Janesville? He's making it all up. And this cheetah—Jeptha Brewster, *you're* making that up! I don't believe it."

Grandma shook her head. "That boy's been between a fever and a fume ever since he heard those new folks were coming. Now they're here all we hear tell about is wild animals and foreigners. John's a nice boy, for all he talks peculiar, but I don't know as I think Jeptha ought to spend so much time with him. There's no telling what notions those people could put in his head."

Miserably Jeptha looked from Grandma to Becky to his mother who had just come into the kitchen.

"The Pomeroys sound interesting to me, Grandma," she said, and put her arm around Jeptha's shoulder. "John's a fine boy and if we find his aunt a little strange, perhaps that's our fault. Here in Janesville we never really get to know outsiders so we judge all of them by ourselves and our neighbors. Maybe *we're* the peculiar ones!"

"But, Mother, a cheetah!" Becky cast her eyes ceilingward. "That just doesn't make sense!"

"It's true, though!" Jeptha's voice was shrill. "Just you wait and see for yourself, Miss Brewster!"

Chapter 3

SCHOOL CLOSED and the whole Penobscot Bay area was color-drenched as flowers bloomed and the waters of the Bay shone sapphire-blue. Big windjammers put out from Plandome Harbor, disappearing across the horizon like great white birds; smaller craft bobbed up and down the bay in a holiday mood; summer homes opened; village streets teemed with tourists. The *Crow's-Nest* parking area was crowded from noon until late evening with cars bearing a variety of license plates, and Jeptha and Becky washed and replenished ash trays in alternating shifts.

At the Pomeroy house there was much grown-up laughter, much coming and going as Auntie Bee's friends from London and New York arrived and departed in a continuous procession of cars. When Jeptha was free he and John would fish off the pilings around the ferry slip, or if the guests and their hostess were away for the day the two boys might play at "harking to Deborah and Mary Ann." As they both had vivid imaginations and both agreed to do whatever the mermaids directed them to do, they sometimes "received" some interesting messages which took them far afield. One of these was the message Jeptha was sure he heard Mary Ann's faint voice whisper, directing them to ride their bicycles up to the Olmstead farm for buttermilk.

To be sure, both the refrigerator at the *Crow's-Nest* and the one in the Pomeroy kitchen were well stocked with buttermilk, but it tasted so much better after the long, hot ride up to Hope, served in thick white mugs with tiny flecks of butter swimming around on the top. Mary Ann probably knew all about Jeptha's longing to see the horses or again she may have wanted John to see the new litter of hound puppies in the corn crib.

The horses unfortunately were far out in the fields, working, so Jeptha had to content himself with sharing John's enthusiasm over the puppies. Mr. Olmstead had promised John one before they were born. Now he crouched over their box, hands on his knees, praying Auntie Bee would say he might have one. His heart was set on the one with four white paws. Already he had named him Socks.

They looked at the pigs and the two new calves and after leaving their empty mugs and their nickels at the back door of the farmhouse, they wandered back to their bicycles. Scuffing along through the high grass on the shady side of the barn, Jeptha stopped and leaning against the side of a truck loaded with empty crates, said, "If you had one wish—just one—what would it be, John?"

John's mind had been very much on the puppies and he almost said, "To have a puppy," but stopped just in time. "I'd rather be with my dad than anything else in the world," he answered.

"But you're going to be in a couple of months, and you've got your aunt." Jeptha was a little hurt. John's wish implied that he was not enjoying being in Janesville. "I think that's a crazy wish," Jeptha added.

His friend, however, did not take offense. "Maybe it is crazy. But you have your own mother. I love Auntie Bee, but she's not the same as a father—or a mother. She has the theatre and lots of people, and that all keeps her busy. She thinks it would be perfectly ripping if I should like to be in the theatre, too. But I'd hate it—and so would Dad. When I grow up I want to be a doctor. If it hadn't been for doctors, just *wonderful* doctors, Dad wouldn't be alive now. I'd like to be able to save people's lives that way."

Jeptha did not say anything. John was lonely, that much he had learned. He understood, for hadn't he missed Father? Didn't he still miss him? But of course, there was Mother, and he was so busy all day long that

the ache had gone out of the missing and only the wonderful memories remained. But suppose he had to live
with only Aunt Mattie? John was asking a question.

"What?"

"What would *you* wish if you could have just one?"
John repeated.

"I'd ask for a horse to ride and ride and ride!" Jeptha
smacked the side of the truck with his open palm with
every "ride" and John laughed to hear the crates rattle.
Then he sobered and sat down suddenly in the high
grass.

"Jeptha, I've got it! I've got it!" he shouted. "I'll
get my wish in September and you'll get yours at the
same time! I say, it's a perfectly smashing idea!"

"Wh-what do you mean?"

"*You go to Arizona with me!* That's what I mean!
You could go to the same school I'm going to out
there, and we'd both ride. Don't you see? It's so sim-
ple, it's made to order, and we can begin making plans
right away!" John had sprung to his feet and was danc-
ing with excitement.

Jeptha felt a shiver of delight run down his spine.
This was too good to be true. Could John possibly
mean it? And even if he did, what would his aunt and
his father think of such an invitation without their
permission? Permission . . . the word stuck in his
heart like a thorn. "Gosh! But no, I don't think Mother
would let me. I mean it's too far away, and besides,

she needs me. No, thanks, John, don't let's think about it. I'd love it more than anything in the world but it's not for me—I mean I can't see it right now," he said in a breathless jumble of words.

But deep within him the hope took root and persisted as they pedaled back downhill to Janesville. Arizona! Horses! Cowboys! John had been away from the States too long to realize to the same degree all that Arizona represented. To Jeptha it combined the very best elements of every dream he had ever known. He remembered so well the day he first had heard John say, "Dad has to live in the western part of America, in Arizona." He remembered the picture that had slid, lightning swift through his mind, the picture of vast prairies dotted with cowboys riding spotted ponies, with a few Indians in blankets sitting in sunny doorways. Arizona! Would he dare ask Mother? No, better not. Once she had said, "You are the man of the house now, Jeptha. I'll depend on you." You couldn't let her know you wanted to go to Arizona after that, could you? When people depended on you, you thought of them first, didn't you?

The boys continued down hill, and turning into the highway, were within a few hundred yards of Auntie Bee's house when Jeptha realized the white-clad figures standing at the curb were Salah and Roshani. They were gesticulating wildly and when they saw the boys approaching, Salah came running to meet them. He was pale and his dark eyes were enormous.

Jeptha and John slid to a stop and jumped from their bicycles. "What's wrong, Salah?" John could not believe this was the usually calm, self-contained Moslem.

"Oh, young master, it is Maghra—Maghra lost—gone!"

"You mean Maghra ran away? Where is memsahib?"

"Memsahib and ladies and gentlemen all go to Portland this morning. Maghra on sun porch. Maybe door not hooked—no one know. Maghra here maybe fifteen minutes ago. Gone now. Where we look?"

John was pale now. This was serious. Auntie Bee had taken pains to keep Maghra's presence in Janesville more or less secret lest the neighbors object to her. There might have been hysteria on the grounds that she was dangerous which was not true, or that she was a menace to livestock which *was* true. Now Maghra had taken matters into her own paws and had vanished.

John tried to think what to do. No point in calling that nice Mr. Peters, the sheriff. He would only frighten Maghra if they did find her and send her bounding off farther than ever. No, he'd have to think of something else.

But Jeptha spoke up quickly. He leaned his bicycle against a tree. "I'd get Salah to drive us in the sta-

tion wagon up toward the Rutherfords' sheep farm,"
he said. "We can watch both sides of the road, and if
Maghra did smell the sheep and go up that way, we
can head her off. If she's around the beach here,
Roshani can get her. She comes to you, doesn't she,
Roshani?"

"Yes, yes, I go look now. Salah, quick, you go in station wagon with young masters." She fluttered up the
drive and disappeared and Salah backed the car out
of the garage. The boys scrambled into the seat beside
him and they started, moving north slowly along the
highway. Cars whizzed by them in both directions and
momentarily they expected to see a yellow streak go
bounding into the road, bringing certain disaster
with it.

Slowly past the big gates of water-front estates they
rolled. Suppose the big cat had gone in to investigate
one of these?

"Shall I try?" Salah suggested, slowing down.

But Jeptha shook his head. "If she's the hunter
Auntie Bee says she is, she'll make for the sheep over
at Rutherfords'. Let's. . . . Look!"

On the left side of the road ran a shallow ditch and
beyond it a strip of deep grass. Beyond this again ran
the white post-and-rail fence separating the broad
meadows of the Rutherford farm from the highway.

Lying in the deep grass, eyes on the flock of sheep and
lambs grazing a hundred feet from her, was Maghra.

She would not creep up on her prey as a lion or leopard would have done. Not at all. She was simply studying her objective. When she had decided which animal she wanted she would either slip under or vault over the fence, launch herself once, twice across the meadow and land on the back of her victim. The kill would be quick and almost instantaneous. Then on to a second. Generations of proud, hunt-trained cheetahs lay behind her; she would not fail.

Salah and the boys knew every second was precious. The Indian drew the car to the side of the road and stopped.

"Let me get her. . . ." Jeptha was breathing hard; he had to get into words somehow all he felt without sounding too sure of himself. "She likes me—you know how she always comes when I'm at the house and we roughhouse. If you go after her, she'll remember she ran away and expect to be scolded or something and she may begin to run. With me maybe she'll only think we're playing. Please!"

"I'll go, too," John interrupted. "Possibly you couldn't hold her even if she did come to you."

"Young master, take care," Salah warned from behind the wheel. "Maghra on hunt, not play today."

Frightened almost out of his wits over what he felt
was a catastrophe due to his own or Roshani's care-
lessness, Salah was torn by conflicting impulses. He
knew he should be the one to try to recover the runaway. On the other hand, he was the only one of the
group who knew how to drive the car, and if Maghra
decided to bolt when he approached, the boys obviously could not follow in the car. Maghra did like
Jeptha, was never so happy as when she was romping
with him or sitting quietly at his feet, her big paws on
his knee while he scratched her head. Here might be
the solution.

It was a chance, a slim one, but perhaps he had better
take it. His teeth chattered and his knuckles were white
as he backed the car slowly to within a few yards of
where Maghra lay.

So intent was the hunter on selecting her prey that
she was not aware of Jeptha, with John following, walking quietly toward her until he stood beside her. Then
she bared her teeth and spit and her long tail lashed
the grass like a whip.

For just a moment Jeptha felt again the sting of
sudden terror he had felt the first time he had seen her
more than a month earlier. She was, after all, a great,
powerful, wild animal and her fangs as she drew back
her lips were frightening. But he pushed the fear far
back in his consciousness, remembering instead that
this was his friend Maghra.

AND THE NEW PEOPLE

He held out his hand, squatting in the grass only a few feet from her. "Hi, baby—hello, girl—how's my Maghra?" he coaxed. "Come on, be a nice girl, come on. . . ." He moved a little closer.

Maghra snarled at him, tossed her head and looked away. The oily scent of the sheep was strong on the wind and she was in no mood for play.

Without raising his voice, Jeptha said to John, "Go, tell Salah to come. I can't hold her alone, but if he'll help I think we can get her in the back of the car. Hurry, but try not to make any noise to get her stirred up. She's pretty mad right now and an exciting noise might start her off. Hurry!" Then he turned back to Maghra.

She was quivering with impatience and with anger at this unforeseen interruption by a friend who should have known better. But the voice she liked went on soothingly and her tail stopped its flailing in the grass.

Jeptha inched forward and slowly, carefully, reached over and scratched her head. She did not seem to mind. Instead, she turned to look at him for an instant, then the golden eyes closed and up from the great chest came the first rumble of a gigantic purr. Jeptha continued stroking her head, scratching her chin, praying Salah would come quickly.

He did, too quickly, with much scrambling down into the ditch then up the far side, much panting and calling on all the gods to witness his predicament.

Maghra was on her feet in an instant, fangs bared.
But Jeptha had her collar now and with a final burst
of energy Salah launched himself at her and slid his
hand through the leather band. There were a few fren-
zied lunges and snarls of rage as the huntress realized
how completely thwarted she was. Then, with John
holding up the rear door of the car, Salah and Jeptha
hauled her up into the station wagon. Jeptha scrambled in after her, still talking soothingly, and sat on
the floor, pulling her down beside him.

In the front seat Salah in an outburst of relief,
talked in Punjabi to John, now and then turning to
nod and grin approvingly at Jeptha. As for Maghra,
she seemed a little ashamed of her escapade and
slapped her tongue again and again as though in ab-
ject apology across Jeptha's hand where it rested on
her leg.

"Let's forget the whole silly business," the slaps
seemed to say. "I thought I wanted to go hunting, but
really I'm much happier just being a big tabby cat!"

The miraculous part of Maghra's misdemeanor was
that, aside from excited voices floating back from one
carload of tourists, shouting, "Look, there's a tiger in
that car!" no one in or around Janesville had seen
her on the road.

Roshani, in despair over her failure to locate the
runaway, was weeping quietly in the kitchen with
Amah trying to comfort her, when the station wagon

turned in the driveway. So by way of celebration there must be ice cream from the deep freeze with ginger sauce for everyone, and for the culprit herself a big bowl of her favorite mash and crab meat.

Jeptha ran home, trundling his bicycle which he couldn't bother to mount, wondering with a glow of pride whether he might not make a good animal trainer instead of a cowboy. Salah and John had seemed to think he had been quite a hero with Maghra. Still, he admitted to himself honestly, she wasn't fierce; she only looked fierce. No, if she were a real leopard. . . . He braced his bicycle against the wall of the house and ran in to tell the family about the morning's adventure.

He found his mother alone in the kitchen. It was almost noon and customers were beginning to drive into the parking area. At this time Mother was usually in the dining room seating people. Today Gertrude, the oldest waitress, seemed to be doing it and Mother was here in the kitchen, covered with Grandma's big apron, directing Myrtle, another waitress, at the oven and stirring the kettle of melted butter as Grandma always did. The whole kitchen looked strange somehow.

"Hi," he greeted them. "Where's everybody? What goes on? Boy, did John and I have fun this morning! Know what? I think. . . ."

"Jeptha," his mother spoke over her shoulder, "do

you think you could watch this kettle for me a moment? Keep stirring the butter—don't let it bubble—take it off if it does. But go wash your hands first. Grandma's sick. Aunt Mattie's upstairs with her. I want to run up a moment."

"Grandma sick?" Already he was at the sink, lathering his hands. "Sure, I'll stir it. There, give me the spoon." His brows were drawn in a worried pucker as he took it from her. "What's the matter with Grandma? She's never sick."

"I don't know, dear. Doctor Benton's coming this afternoon. But with Becky in Dark Harbor, my hands are pretty full. I don't want to call her back because, after all, she's just gone and she's been looking forward all spring to these weeks with the Shepherd girls. Just stir for a few minutes, son. I'll be right back."

Jeptha stirred. He had watched Grandma do it too often not to be competent himself. But Grandma sick! Somehow you never thought of her in connection with illness. She'd probably be down for supper. He had so much to tell the whole family that it seemed a pity any member should miss it. Still, when there was sickness you did not talk about things like animal training or Arizona.

The butter began to bubble, and just as he had seen Grandma do, he set the kettle far back on the range and put the little copper bowls in a row on the table beside it. Arizona—spotted ponies—they seemed very far away.

When Doctor Benton came he did not stay very long. Shortly after he left the ambulance arrived, and with Mother and Aunt Mattie beside her, Grandma was taken to the hospital in Plandome. Hattie Pringle came to help the cook in the kitchen that afternoon and evening, and then Mother came back looking very white and tired. Aunt Mattie who always had lived with her cousins, the Pringles, over the post office, slept at Jeptha's house that night and it was she who answered the telephone when it rang at dawn the next morning. Grandma had died in her sleep.

Chapter 4

JEPTHA COULD not believe it: that he never would see Grandma again, and in the days that followed he was a very solemn, bewildered boy. John, who had been too young to remember much of his own bereavement when his mother died, was little help. Auntie Bee crossed the road to bring flowers from her garden and lingered on to chat with Jeptha's mother whom she found quite different from what she had expected. A few evenings later she brought her five house guests to the *Crow's-Nest* for one of its famous lobster dinners and greeted Mrs. Brewster as an old friend.

Becky, from the kitchen, was sorry she and not Gertrude was filling water glasses. Jeptha had told the truth; John's aunt was *the* Beatrice Pomeroy and her guests, Becky decided, looked very distinguished. Jeptha had all the luck. He had been the one who had been interested in the new people even before they had arrived.

True, there had been John who had become his
friend, but on the other hand, if she, Becky, had been
interested, she could have made herself valuable in
some way to Miss Pomeroy and might even have im-
pressed her with her acting. Hadn't she played an im-
portant part in the school play? And hadn't the coach
said she showed "marked talent"? Still it had to be
Jeptha who had become the invaluable one—he and
his love for an old cheetah!

Becky tossed her sleek brown pony tail and decided
life was dreadfully unfair. Becky at fourteen had def-
inite views about many things. There was Grandma's
apartment upstairs, for instance. Grandma and Grandpa had chosen to keep two large comfortable rooms
and a bath on the second floor of the *Crow's-Nest* for
their own use. Becky, Jeptha, and their mother had
the rooms on the first floor adjoining the big public
dining room. Now with both Grandma and Grandpa
gone, Becky saw no reason why their suite should not
be hers. It would be such fun to replace the dark old
furniture with something light, put bright cretonne
at the windows, move her record player and radio up
there and really have a little apartment of her own.
She would speak to Mother about it the first chance
she had.

Another plan of Becky's was to leave Janesville at
the first possible moment. The county high school was
all very well, but the Shepherd girls were going to

Boston to school next winter, so why shouldn't she? After all, hadn't Mother gone to Chicago University? Jeptha might be happy here, but then he was a boy. So Becky dreamed in the kitchen as she turned the switch on the potato masher.

The Fourth of July dawned sparkling and cool. Auntie Bee and her guests alternated between swimming off the little sandy beach at the end of the garden and sun-bathing on the lawn. John in brand new scarlet bathing trunks and Jeptha in his faded blue ones, joined the boys and girls at the public bathing beach a block away. John was learning to swim though he did not particularly enjoy it.

This morning the blue water of the bay was ruffled with whitecaps and the water was cold. Frank Pringle's brother, Obed, going out to check his lobster traps, hailed the boys as he passed.

"Want to come along for the ride, kids?" he called. "It'll be bumpy in this wind, but all the more fun."

"Will you wait 'til I ask Mother?" Jeptha turned to John. "Want to go? It'll be fun and you can see the live lobsters, too. Want to?"

"I'll wait for you down at the slip." Obed waved toward it. "If you can't go, just wig-wag and I'll start off and. . . ." He added something that was blown away by the wind, and Jeptha raced off up the road.

John did not in the least want to go. He was cold and the very thought of bobbing about in Obed's

launch through the choppy seas turned him sick. But
he dreaded having Jeptha think him a coward, so he
nodded. "Yes, if your mother lets you go I know
Auntie Bee won't mind. I'd love to go."

Jeptha came tearing back, grinning with delight.
"Mother said yes," he shouted. "Only I've got to be
back by noon to help at home—there's going to be a
crowd today. Come on, John."

They ran down the beach hand in hand, Jeptha
so sturdy, the color of maple sugar, John a slender,
freckled, delicately made boy who smiled anxiously,
determinedly as he ran. Obed was waiting at the slip,
his gasoline motor put-putting importantly. He helped
the boys in, warning them not to tangle with the gear
and to hold fast.

The bay was dotted with sail boats, dories, pea pods,
launches, every imaginable type of small craft, and
against the distant line of a long narrow island, a big
freighter moved majestically toward Bangor, nodding,
bowing in the gusty swells. Obed's little craft plunged
along, spray flying across its bow. Now it careened into
a valley of blue water, again it rode a dizzy peak, and
Jeptha, worthy seaman that he was, wondered why he
had not worn his oilskins, why he had not seen to it
that John was protected from the icy water pouring
over them.

Obed turned to look back at them. "I hollered to
you kids to wear your oilskins," he shouted. "Guess

you didn't hear me. 'Fraid you'll ketch cold." The launch slid smoothly up a mountain of water, rolled, then plummeted down the other side, and as it did, there was a flash of scarlet over its side.

For an instant Jeptha saw John's dark head bob to the surface, then disappear again. Horror held him, then he was in the water, choking, thrashing blindly at first, then shaking the water from his eyes, trying to locate John. Once he thought he spied him, heard Obed's frantic cry, and found himself alone in an oily curve of the sea. Then, ten feet from him, he glimpsed the dark head again. John was swimming, thrashing arms and legs, trying to keep his head above water. Obed was maneuvering the boat toward them

Jeptha struck out toward John's flying arms and caught one of them. "Hey, hang onto my shoulder," he yelled. "Don't pull down—just hang on. That's right. Let's go!" His own body was beginning to feel strangely numb as he circled about in the icy water trying to get within reach of Obed's outstretched hand.

The little boat dodged, swung crazily, rolled dangerously as Obed leaned from it. He caught Jeptha's wrist with one hand and with the other managed to grab John's arm. Jeptha pulled himself up and over into the boat and Obed hauled John in after him. Obed wrapped his oilskin around John who was blue

and made Jeptha put on his sweater. Then he started
back to shore.

Bathers on the beach had seen the accident and were
waiting with blankets.

"Oh, gosh, I'm okay," Jeptha snorted shamefacedly. "I've got to get home." He wanted to see how John was making out and he wished people would stop making such a fuss. He started toward John but his knees buckled and he sat down suddenly, very sick at his stomach.

John, still in the oilskins, tried to sit up but abandoned the idea after a second try. "I'm awfully sorry," he said shakily, looking up at Obed. "It was my own fault. I thought I was hanging on but I just slid over the side before I knew what was happening. Is Jeptha all right? He saved me. Y-yes, y-yes, t-thank you, I'm quite all right, j-j-just c-c-cold." His lips were blue, his body jerked spasmodically and his teeth chattered as chill after chill shook him. Obed picked him up, and with Jeptha, still pallid but determined at his heels, carried him home.

At first John seemed to be all right. Obediently he got into a scalding bath, went to bed and swallowed the hot milk laced with brandy that Auntie Bee insisted he drink. But by mid-afternoon his cheeks were flushed and he admitted his chest and back ached. So again Doctor Benton's car stopped in the neighborhood and again his visit was short.

"This boy will be much better off in the hospital, Miss Pomeroy," he said as he closed his bag. "He's running a high fever and he's going to need all the care day and night that we can give him. I'll send the ambulance right out."

With that he was gone, and Auntie Bee, her guests, her Oriental trappings and Maghra forgotten, turned to Jeptha's mother. "My dear, tell me what to do!" she begged. "You have a boy of your own. In the years John's been with me he's never been ill aside from an occasional bout with malaria or an infected insect bite when we were in India. I'm so terribly frightened. You see, his father wanted me to bring him home last winter but the play . . . well, that's neither here nor there. Do you think I ought to send for him, that is for my brother Jack, John's father?"

Mrs. Brewster hesitated, then, "He's so far away and it seems a pity to alarm him. Had you thought of phoning him? You might mention that John is ill following a drenching. That would at least warn him, and you could say you would keep in touch with him. Then if John's condition worsens he would at least be prepared for another call. I think it is what I would do. I feel so guilty! If I had realized what a high sea was running I *never* would have consented to letting the boys go out in the first place. I blame myself. . . ."

"You'll do nothing of the sort!" Auntie Bee impulsively took both her hands. "Why didn't I think of telephoning? You've been a tremendous help. I'll do it this instant."

Jeptha, too, had been put to bed much against his

will. When evening came he lay in the dark listening
to the jubilant sounds coming from the beach, the
snarl and boom of fireworks, the shrieks and laughter
of people gathered there to watch them; and his heart
was heavy. Everything had been such fun for a while
after John came. Then, only a few weeks ago Grandma
had died and now John—he dared not think farther,
but his eyes smarted in the dark and his chest heaved
mightily as he choked back sobs. John was the closest
friend he had ever known; he was like a brother, a
twin brother, almost. They had discovered that
Jeptha's birthday had been in April and John's would
be in August.

Why had they gone out in Obed's danged old boat?
Jeptha berated himself. Why hadn't he warned John
about the way it rolled and how you had to hang on
tight in a heavy sea? Now John would hate Janesville
more than ever; now when he went to Arizona he
would never want to think of it again. If only the hospital were closer he could go and sit with John tonight. No, Mother wouldn't let him do that, of course,
but anyway he'd go the very first thing in the morning.
He might even go up to Mr. Olmstead's and see if he
could have the pup John liked so much and take it
with him. Yes, that's what he'd do! So at last he fell
asleep.

The big plane from New York touched down and

came to a graceful stop at the Rockland airport. The tall man in tweeds whose dark hair was touched with gray at the temples and whose mouth was set in grim, hard lines, tossed his newspaper to the seat beside him, unfastened his seat belt and got up. Other passengers were greeting friends, scattering to collect their luggage and be off. He claimed his own bags and hailed a cab.

"I want to go to the Plandome hospital," he told the driver. "I imagine you know where it is? I'm a stranger here."

"Ayah." The ruddy-faced driver picked up his luggage and stored it on the front seat. "Hope you've got no sick kin there. Always sad to have sick kin, I say."

The newcomer got in, leaned back and closed his eyes. "Yes, I have a sick boy there. Pneumonia. He nearly drowned the other day in the bay out at Janesville Beach and. . . ."

"Oh, now then, that 'd likely be the lad that fell out of Obed Pringle's boat. Him and young Jeptha Brewster went out in Obed's lobster boat in a heavy sea and as I hear it the one little fellow went over the side and Jeptha in after him. Wonder they both didn't ketch the pneumonia—cold it was, the Fourth. Your boy lives with that actress lady bought or rented the Custer place, hm?"

"The lady, Miss Pomeroy, is my sister. As I see it,

it was one of those accidents no one is to blame for. But I'm anxious."

"That you must be, sir. Well, we'll be there in about fifteen minutes. They been fixin' th' roads all up through here goin' on two years now and it's kept things pretty much tore up, so you'll have to excuse the bumps."

There was a silence while John's father alternately sat with closed tired eyes or briefly watched the woods and fields flash by with here and there a patch of distant water. The long flight east from Arizona the previous day and the weight of anxiety on his heart had left Jack Pomeroy indifferent to bad roads and fine scenery alike. But his driver, by nature a curious man, had another question.

"Not meaning to give offense, sir," he observed in the rear view mirror, "but folks say the lady, your sister, keeps a real live tiger—no, leopard it is—right in her house. Now I'd call that downright dangerous, 'specially with children around. Brother o' mine lives out at the Beach and he was tellin' me that at the last Town Meetin' there was some talk o' gettin' up a protest like and servin' it, the leopard bein' a menace to life. I'm not one to mix in with what ain't my business but seems to me they got somethin' there. Suppose that leopard was to get loose in th' village and begin runnin' wild. Lot o' people could be hurt, no doubt about it, ayah. . . ."

John's father smiled patiently. "No, there isn't any danger. You see, the animal isn't a leopard; it's a cheetah and harmless as a pussy cat."

"But look, now, not wanting to differ with you, you understand, why would anybody want a big dangerous lookin' thing like that around?"

"Really, I wouldn't know. The only way I can explain it is that the lady has temperament."

"Fever like?"

"Well, yes, in a manner of speaking. Ah, we seem to be here. Thank you very much. I've taken down your company's number and if I need you later I'll call."

He collected his bags, paid the still mystified driver and ran up the broad, shallow steps of the hospital. At the desk he was directed to the second floor, and so it was that he came upon Auntie Bee reading a magazine beside an open window in the hall.

She did not see him until he stood looking down at her. Then she looked up and the magazine slid from her lap as he put his arms around her.

"Jack, oh, Jack, darling, you came! You came!" was all she could murmur over and over again.

"How is he? Can I see him, Bee? Is it very bad? After you called the other day I found I couldn't stand the uncertainty, so here I am."

"He's doing as well as can be expected from one who is allergic to antibiotics. That has made it so very

hard. He simply cannot take them. Doctor Benton
thinks the crisis will come within the next forty-eight
hours. Then we'll know more. But I wouldn't try to
see John now, at least not without the doctor's sanc-
tion. Everything that can be done to help is being
done. The nurses are wonderful and our neighbors
out at the Beach are incredibly kind. I called you
again yesterday but they said at the ranch that you
were gone. So I've been expecting you."

"But what possible harm could it do for me just to
look at him a moment?"

"Just this, Jack—try to be reasonable—it's been four
years since he saw you and he might not recognize
you. If that were the case he might be frightened—a
stranger suddenly in his room. If he did recognize
you, the excitement would be very bad. You have no
idea, Jack, what you mean to that boy! Your letters,
the things you've sent him, these are sacred treasures,
and since he's known he was actually going to live with
you, he's been counting the days. He and his friend
Jeptha Brewster spend hours with the atlas pointing
out spots on the state of Arizona to each other where
they think the ranch may be. Oh, here is Doctor
Benton!"

The two men liked each other instantly. The doctor
went into John's room and returned almost at once.
"He's asleep," he said, "so go in, but if he does waken

just come out and I'll go in. I doubt that John will waken, though."

So Jack Pomeroy tiptoed into the sick room, circled the starched nurse who sat at the bedside, and looked down at his son. How he had grown! Yet he seemed painfully thin and in his troubled sleep a deep frown gave to his young face the look of an old man. His father sighed, longing to touch the dark curls on the pillow, wondering miserably as he had so often, whether his plan to leave his son in his aunt's care while he recovered his own health in the West had been such a good plan after all. This fragile looking boy seemed so desperately in need of security and all the things that came with it, like regular wholesome meals, plenty of sleep, out-of-doors living the year round. Well, he should have them all, God willing. Knowing sister Bee's erratic notions, how could he have been foolish enough to trust John to her care? He had been very sick himself four years ago and broken-hearted over his wife's death. *Someone* had to be made responsible for John's care, and Bee did love him deeply in her own strange way. Still. . . .

The doctor advised that the Pomeroys go home as nothing could be gained by their staying, but Jack Pomeroy demurred. "If you have a vacant room, Doctor, even a cot in a corridor somewhere, I'd like to be here near John if possible. I've been away from him far too long as it is."

Auntie Bee objected. Now that the responsibility had slipped from her own shoulders to her brother's much of her concern had vanished with it. "But he's in such good hands, Jack. Besides, I want to have you to myself this evening. I want to show you off to my guests. You'll love the Clarks and Jimmy Blaine, the *most.* . . ."

"My dear Bee," there was exasperation in the father's voice, "the only thing—please try to understand this—the *only* thing that interests me is John's condition. We'll have plenty of time for confabing once I know he is well again. As for the Clarks and Jimmy whatever-his-name-is, I can see them later, too. I'm staying here tonight if Doctor Benton will let me."

So Auntie Bee drove off, her cheeks very rosy with indignation, and John's father settled down in a room not far from his son's to keep his vigil. Exhausted after sleepless nights and his flight east, he fell asleep almost at once, waking only in the early evening when an orderly brought him coffee and sandwiches. The evening passed, midnight came and went. He walked the corridor, stopped at the window to study the tree-tops moving against the stars.

John, poor little tyke, he thought, carted around the world by a beautiful, temperamental woman whose only interest in little boys was that they must be well-mannered and decorative. This lung of mine has been healed for almost three years and yet I've told myself the boy was better off in what I called "a healthy atmosphere." Healthy, my hat! With the ranch to roam over and the purest air on earth to breathe, with a good school within riding distance, what on earth have I been thinking of to leave him with Bee so long? She's a woman, yes, "giving him a woman's care" as the old-fashioned novels used to say, but what care *did* she actually give him? Her career came first. Whatever time was left over may have been given to John; still, I believe to carry out the British tradition, there was an Amah for him, an Indian nurse for a six-year-old boy! And she's probably still there to lend atmosphere! What an unmitigated, blundering fool I've been! What would John's mother have thought! How ashamed of me she would have been!

He buried his face in his hands, trying to pray, scarcely daring to. Then a nurse touched his arm.

Chapter 5

JOHN ROSE and fell and rose again in the great swells of boiling fog through which his boat was carrying him. The heat was unbearable and somewhere Jeptha's voice kept calling, "Hang on to my shoulder, John, and we'll swim out to the spotted ponies." Only when you obeyed, the spotted ponies were lobster traps and in some strange way you managed to get into one of them and could not get out.

The harder you thrashed your arms about, the more insistent was the voice—not Jeptha's now—saying quietly, "Keep your arms down, John, that's a good boy. You must not push the covers down so." Then the hot fog would close in again. You were very thirsty and tried to ask for water, but your voice refused to reach the level of your lips and stayed stubbornly in your throat.

On and on through the boiling fog John went, crying now and ashamed of crying, and then he must have fallen asleep. Presently he opened his eyes and found he was not bobbing any more and that by some means he had managed to get out of the lobster trap. Maybe he was back in Obed's boat, but if that were true the sea was very calm. Perhaps he was adrift somewhere far out in the bay, moving toward the open sea. He turned his head ever so slightly and found to his amazement and joy that he was lying quietly in a bed. How then could his face be so clammy and wet? Perspiration lay in pools along the hollow of his throat and beneath his knees. His pajamas clung to him in soggy lengths; his pillow was wet.

Fingers were on his wrist and a voice he remembered vaguely as Doctor Benton's said, "Good-morning, John. How do you feel this morning?"

For a moment he could not answer. He was still confused by this sudden arrival in a bed after his wild ride in the lobster trap, and words still stopped just short of his lips. He could only smile a little sheepishly and by a great effort whisper, "Okay, sir. That was a cracking ride I had!" Then he fell asleep again, this time not to dream, and to wake in dry clothes and with a dry, cool pillow under his head. A little later a cup of broth tasted delicious and Doctor Benton came to stand beside him and say in his quiet voice,

"Since you have been such a good sailor about taking your broth, I have a little surprise for you. You

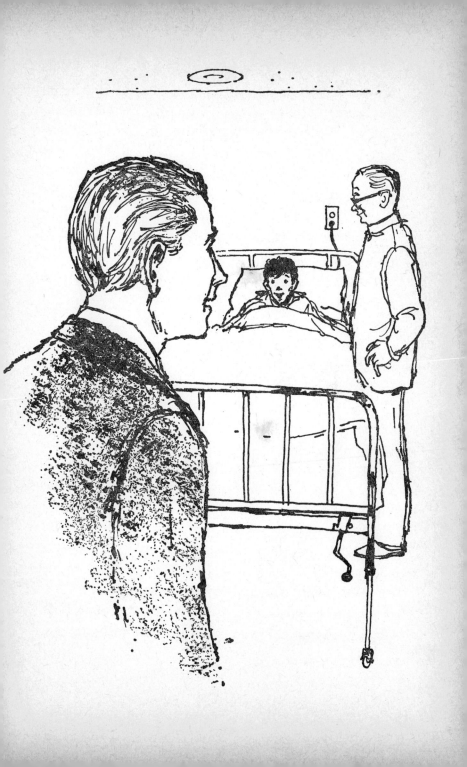

have a visitor and you may see him for just five minutes. Promise not to ask for more?"

John nodded, grinning happily. "It's that Jeptha, I
know!"

And then a tall man stood in the doorway, smiling
at him and his heart began pounding as though it
would burst right through his pajama jacket. "Dad!
Dad! Dad!" No other words would come as he tried to
told up his arms and failed.

He felt himself held against a rough tweed coat and
heard a voice he had dreamed of across the years saying, "John, my son, my boy, my little boy!"

When he would have tried to talk his father laid a
finger on his lips. "They're giving us only five minutes
today," he cautioned, "but I'll be back first thing to-
morrow morning. Then we can begin making plans for
that trip we're going to take back to *Blue Feather
Ranch* in Arizona. No more talking today, old fellow."
He kissed John, hugged him again and settled him
back on his pillow and backed out, smiling, as the
nurse entered.

His own heart bursting with happiness, he walked
blindly into a pretty woman and a boy who had just
turned away from the floor nurse's desk.

"There's Mr. Pomeroy now!" the nurse exclaimed
as the colliding group made laughing apologies. "Mrs.
Brewster," she joined them, "this is John's father, and

Mr. Pomeroy, this is Jeptha, the boy we all feel we owe a lot to."

Jeptha scuffed and looked embarrassed, but remembered his manners in time and held out his hand. John's dad! Was he ever the nice looking man! Nicer even than his picture! He listened without actually hearing while his mother and John's father talked. He gathered that John was better but that there wasn't a chance he could so much as peep in at the door.

"Unless complications develop," Mr. Pomeroy was saying, "we should have the boy back to normal within a few days."

"Jeptha and I came into Plandome to get shoes," his mother was explaining, "and I couldn't resist stopping at the hospital to hear for myself how John was doing. We've grown very, very fond of that boy of yours, Mr. Pomeroy, and we're going to miss him terribly when he leaves us in the fall. By the way, I have my car downstairs. Can I run you out to the Beach? We're just across the road from your sister's, you know."

Jeptha saw Mr. Pomeroy hesitate. "You're so kind," he said finally. "I must look like a tramp. What I thought I would do would be to stay in Plandome at the Inn. My sister's house is full of guests and I'm frankly too tired to face them. Besides, I doubt she has room to put me up."

"Come to our house," Jeptha invited hospitably. "We've got lots of room, haven't we, Mother? Grandma's bedroom and sitting room and bathroom and everything."

He knew he had made a mistake when he saw his mother's cheeks turn very pink, but wasn't quite sure what the mistake was until he heard her embarrassed laugh and heard her say, "Of course we'd enjoy having Mr. Pomeroy use Grandma's rooms if he would care to, dear, but you see, we might offend Miss Pomeroy by whisking a member of her own family away from her like that. One does not do that, you know." To Mr. Pomeroy she added, "We'd be happy, indeed, to have both you and John when he is able. My mother-in-law's suite on our second floor is vacant, and as we, that is my sister-in-law, the children and I use the first floor which is entirely separate, you would be completely independent of us and certainly no trouble. But I'd rather the suggestion came from Miss Pomeroy. She has heard me say I might rent the second floor suite so it would be perfectly natural for her to think of it."

Jeptha did not know when he had enjoyed the familiar ride from Plandome to the Beach so much. His heart sang. John was better and he might be living right in his house, and John's father, too! Now if they could bring Maghra with them everything would be perfect.

Thinking aloud, he said as they swung down along Route One, skirting the bay, "Maghra'd like to be at our house, too, I know, at least while the company is at Auntie Bee's. That man, Jimmy, pretends Maghra's a tiger and he's a wild animal trainer and he shoots off a cap pistol and pokes a kitchen chair at her, and everybody laughs and claps. And Maghra's scared and goes off and cries. John and I don't like it and. . . ."

"That will do, son." Mother really looked cross now. "Never mind about Maghra. No one is hurting her. Miss Pomeroy wouldn't permit that. And as for having her at the *Crow's-Nest,* how long do you think we'd remain open if we had a cheetah on the place?"

"You see, Jeptha," John's father laughed good-naturedly, "wild Westerners are one thing but wild animals are another. Personally, if I had my way, we'd ship poor Maghra back to India and turn her out in the open where she belongs. Maybe we can work it out somehow. I'd send her to Arizona but I'm afraid of the damage she might do to livestock. We'll see. Things have a way of working out."

Things certainly seemed to. Jeptha was still trying on the new shoes when the telephone rang and Auntie Bee asked to speak to Mother. *Would* she consider renting to John's father for the rest of July and possibly a week or so in August the suite she had mentioned recently? Her own house would be filled with guests for weeks as she was beginning rehearsals—her manager would be there as well—and John would need quiet and "brother Jack seems so bored with it all."

Would dear Mrs. Brewster do her this inestimable favor?

Mother explained that it was no favor and went to hull berries for shortcake. Jeptha pranced gleefully about in his slippery new shoes until he collided with the TV and sat down hard. He did not care, though. John and his father were coming to live at their house! Oh, boy!

He went upstairs with Mr. Pomeroy when Mother showed him the rooms he and John would have, pointed out the view of the mountains John would get from his window and ended by bringing up his favorite fishing rod to stand in the corner.

"John doesn't care so much for fishing," he admitted, "but maybe leaving tackle around he might get up some sort of interest. And I know he wants one of the Olmsteads' puppies, so could we. . . ."

"Jeptha!" Mother was laughing, but you knew she thought you talked too much. "Let Mr. Pomeroy and John make their own decision about the puppy. Come, Becky's alone with the butter patties to make and it is getting late. You have your job, you know."

"I hope you will be comfortable, Mr. Pomeroy," she added, "and if you need anything just ring. The bell is connected with the kitchen. Come, son." She put her arm around Jeptha's shoulder and steered him to the door.

He would have loved to stay but he knew Becky

was apt to spoil more butter patties than she made perfect ones. Her *"Crow's-Nest"* on the patty usually read " 's-Nes" and that was bad. He sighed deeply, trying to think of one last excuse to stay a little longer, and clattered downstairs after his mother.

For several minutes after Jeptha and his mother left, Jack Pomeroy sat on the edge of the big four-poster bed staring out at the sea, yet seeing nothing. How could a world change so completely in a few hours, he thought? For days he had felt alone both in his agony of mind over John and then in his joy at the crisis safely passed. No one, his sister least of all, had seemed to care what became of them. They were alone and far from the home John had dreamed of so long—strangers in a strange land. Jack Pomeroy always had thought of himself as a man who could cope with almost any situation, but the terrible feeling of *aloneness* that had swept over him in the little Maine community was beyond anything he ever had known.

Then out of the blue had come a woman who was gentle and understanding and a boy offering his most prized possession, anxious only that John should be happy. As by magic the hard bands of loneliness and uncertainty that had been closing tighter and tighter about his heart began to relax. The breeze coming in the window was sweet with the smell of the sea, the sunlight lay golden across the sill.

He stood up, whistling softly and began unpacking

his bags. Then he showered and returned to the bed to enjoy the first deep sleep he had known in what seemed a lifetime. As he drifted off, the sharp report of a cap pistol came faintly from across the road, followed by much laughter and applause.

Another week passed and several times Jeptha rode into the hospital to bring John the latest news from Janesville Beach. John was impatient to be out of the hospital and was overjoyed to hear of the move to the *Crow's-Nest*.

"When I come back," he told Jeptha, "maybe Dad will go with us up to the Olmsteads' to see the pups. When he sees how cute they are I'm sure he'll let me have Socks, don't you think so?"

"Ayah, he'll let you have most anything you want, I guess."

One day John's father sat back from the jigsaw puzzle they had been working over and said casually, "You're very fond of Jeptha, aren't you, son?"

John nodded and laid down the piece he had just picked up. "He's the very best chap I've ever known, Dad," he answered slowly. "I wish he was my brother."

His father smiled. "How do you feel about Becky?"

"Oh, Becky's quite all right, a bit silly, but then all girls are, you know."

"Do you think so? Maybe you're right. And how about Jeptha's mother, Mrs. Brewster?"

John thought this over for some seconds, trying to straighten out a snarl in his usually straightforward answers. "Well, Dad," he said at last, "I don't quite know how to say it. Auntie Bee is supposed to be beautiful—I fancy she is, rather. But Mrs. Brewster is more what I'd call beautiful. For one thing, she doesn't always make you feel like a—a baby. She doesn't ask you questions and then sort of laugh when you answer her. She talks to you as if you were grown up, like the time she asked me what I thought I'd like to be when I grew up and I said a grocer. . . ."

"*A grocer,* John? Now why in the world would you want to be a grocer?"

"Because everybody has to eat and if you're clever and have just the nippiest sort of grocery store you know how to have, people are bound to come to your store and before long you'll be rich. That's what I told Mrs. Brewster, though now I think I'd rather be a doctor, and she didn't laugh. She said, 'It sounds like a very intelligent plan, John.' That's what I mean about thinking she's beautiful. She makes you like to talk to her. I fancy it's the same thing, isn't it?"

His father studied the serious young face for a long moment. "I guess you're right, son, I guess you really are," he said.

Early August came and John was taking his first short rides on his bicycle. He was eating vast amounts of rare steak, drinking quarts of milk, and one day

Jeptha pounded him on the back and declared, "Know what, John? If you get just one ounce fatter you'll bust that new sweater your father got for you last week sure as anything!"

John was far from fat but he had lost his hospital pallor and his thin young frame was filling out. Jeptha himself was busier than ever. So was Becky, and as for Mrs. Brewster, when evening came she had scarcely the energy at nine o'clock to check the cash and lock the front door. Aunt Mattie had suddenly decided to be a September bride, and though her sober thirty-nine-year-old heart should have counseled more wisdom and consideration, she skimmed through her work with all the giddy abandon of an eighteen-year-old. Watching her dreamily spilling cream on a clean table cloth, her sister-in-law was often close to tears of exasperation.

Jack Pomeroy had acquired a sturdy second-hand car and almost every day he and the two boys and frequently Becky, too, went for morning picnics up in the hills, cooking their steaks on an open fire and returning, ash-streaked and happy in the late afternoon. Becky and Jeptha always vanished for baths and clean clothes and went promptly to the kitchen to take up their dinner-time work.

John and his father looked after them ruefully; and one evening as Mrs. Brewster was locking the front door, Jack Pomeroy came in through the kitchen.

"Look—forgive me," he began hesitantly, "but I cannot help seeing how tired you are. It's been such a hot day and I think you need a little fresh air and relaxation. Come for a ride. It will do you good. Miss Mattie's here to see that the children are all right. Come on—just for an hour. Do come!"

Rebecca Brewster was afraid for one horrible moment that she had not heard right. It had been almost three years since any man had been concerned about her welfare and this man was so fine, so considerate.

"I'd like to," she said. "Just let me tell Becky and Jeptha and pick up a sweater."

She had not realized quite how exhausted she was until she leaned back in the comfortable seat, letting the soft night wind lift her moist hair from her forehead, the day's responsibilities slipping away. They spoke of familiar things. She told John's father of the problems of running a popular shore dinner restaurant, of her shortage of help and Mattie's impending marriage which would make it even more acute. She spoke of her reluctance at having the children so much a part of the problem yet her desire to give them a sense of responsibility in a matter which concerned them all.

He spoke of *Blue Feather Ranch,* of the cattle and cattle diseases, of the new addition to the ranch house built the past year, of Indian ceremonies and rodeos. When they returned, her weariness had vanished and they were laughing like a pair of high school students over an amusing anecdote of her telling. As she lit the lamp on her night table, Becky's sleepy voice from the next room reminded her, "Aunt Mattie said she didn't think you would mind if we had ice cream, Jeptha, John, and I, so we did. Was it O.K.?"

"O.K., darling. Good night." Rebecca Brewster lay for a long time staring into the darkness. Life, progress, time, these colored one's days. She had known happiness and sorrow and hard work; her children were children any mother could be proud of. Now into their little group had come a motherless boy whom they loved and his father who already was endearing himself to them all. What form would the final picture take? Thinking of these things, Jeptha's mother fell asleep.

John's father had given his permission for John to have Socks and as he was obliged to fly to New York on a day's business later the same week, the boys went up to the Olmstead farm alone to look at the puppies. None had been taken as yet, but they had been weaned and were ready for new homes whenever they were wanted. John found Socks without any trouble and buried his face in the pup's soft neck.

"Is it all right if I take him now, Mr. Olmstead?" he queried. Such a gift was almost beyond belief. To Jeptha a hound pup was just another farm animal, to be cared for and loved, to be sure, but nothing to grow excited about. Now Maghra—or a spotted pony!

Mr. Olmstead wiped his hands on his overalls. "Well, now, boy," the words came deliberately, "I been hearin' something 'bout you—'bout your house, you might say. Young Rudie Betsford was tellin' my boy that your folks keep a live leopard at your house —eats young animals, he says. Says I'd better not let any of my pups get nigh your place. What do you say to that, young feller?"

John held the puppy tighter. "It's not true, sir. My aunt does have a cheetah but it's harmless as a kitten. It would love this puppy—but not to eat."

"That I'd want to see! Betsfords is kin o' mine and they don't lie."

"Rudie does!" Jeptha had not meant to speak, but the words just flew from him. "Come up now, Mr. Olmstead, right *now,* and see if I'm not telling the truth!"

Mr. Olmstead looked at the sun. "Gettin' on to noon, dinner time," he observed. "If 't was anybody but your pa's boy, Jeptha Brewster, I'd give you the wallopin' of your life for callin' Rudie a liar. But come on, I got the jeep here. You follow me on your bikes. I want to see this here leopard. Is it chained up? Bring the pup along, young feller. No sense goin' way back to the barn with it. Now come on, let's go. I got to be getting back for dinner."

The boys followed the rusty Olmstead jeep down the hill, across the highway, and drew up with a flourish before Auntie Bee's house. Mr. Olmstead, crossing the lawn, saw a golden-haired goddess in shorts and sweater on the screened porch declaiming to a young man, also in shorts and wearing a scraggy black beard, "Come, darling, we're not wanted here—no, drat it, that's wrong! Come darling, they don't want us here. Come to me and we will leave this rotting pile and find happiness in Algeria!"

The bearded one crushed her face against his beard and from somewhere inside the house a voice screamed, "Kiss me, darling! God save the Queen! Ring down the curtain!"

"Oh, shut up, Kirby!" shouted the goddess, wiping her mouth on her sleeve. "Oh—hello, boys? Who—er—is our visitor?" She advanced and opened the screen door. "Won't you come in, Mr.—er—?"

"Olmstead, ma'am. I come to see about the leopard. Your son . . ."

"Nephew. . . ."

"Nephew wants one of our pups and I heard you got a live leopard here. Now, looks to me like the place is a kind o' crazy house even without th' leopard. Who's that woman yellin' so?"

As Kirby at that moment flung out a final maudlin, "Hello, sweet! God save the Queen!" and the "leopard" sauntered out from the house to sniff his boots,

Mr. Olmstead looked not only increasingly bewildered but a little sick.

The goddess clapped her hands and a turbaned Moslem appeared in the doorway. "Bring ginger ale, Salah. Boys, there's a box of candy inside on the piano." Then she turned to Mr. Olmstead, rigid in his chair, white even under his tan. "I do hope you will forgive us and try to understand, Mr. Olmstead. We are rehearsing a play in which I am to appear in San Francisco in another month or so. That accounts for the—er—the love scene you just witnessed. Ah, Salah, open the bottles and pass a glass to the gentleman. . . . As for the voice you heard, that was my parrot. His repertory is not long so he repeats. As for Maghra, come here, darling."

Maghra gave up the minute inspection of Mr. Olmstead's boots and padded over to put her head in Auntie Bee's lap. "You can see she is as harmless as—as that puppy John has. Bring it here, John."

John and Jeptha, both rather obviously munching chocolate covered caramels, emerged from the house and John held out the puppy to Maghra. She sniffed it all over very carefully and from her chest came the deep, contented rumble of her purr. Then she began a systematic lapping. Socks was going to be clean as he never had been clean before. It looked as though his floppy brown ears might be torn from his head, as though he would be permanently blinded as Maghra's

thwarted maternity unleashed itself on what she considered his well being. Socks was her child and she adored him. When he had been polished to her satisfaction, she relinquished him to John, but followed him about, purring a little sadly.

"Well, ma'am, it beats me," Mr. Olmstead admitted, setting his empty glass on the floor beside him. "I'd never have believed it, no siree, but I've seen it with my own eyes. The boy can have the pup. Ayah, Jeptha, I'm not sayin' you're the whole way right, but you ain't so wrong, boy, either!" He stomped off across the lawn and John held Socks tighter as Auntie Bee again struck her pose.

"Come on, Jimmy, try it once more. 'Come, darling, they don't want us here. . . .' "

Chapter 6

AUGUST BLANKETED most of the country with withering heat. The newspapers carried headlines telling the number of deaths in various cities due to heat prostration and sunstroke. Up along the shores of Penobscot Bay the temperature remained in the seventies and on two memorable days rose to eighty-five. The air was winy with the rich scents of late summer, and as the month wore on, smoke from fireplaces curled up lazily after nightfall.

Auntie Bee's house continued to bulge with ever oncoming guests. Jimmy and his beard left for a time but returned; rehearsals continued; Maghra grieved over Socks's long absences and cried in unashamed delight when he put in an all-too-brief appearance. Then she would scrub him thoroughly, lecture him with affectionate little cuffings, and purr over him until, drugged by the rhythmic rumble, he would fall asleep against her soft side.

These were the happiest days of the summer, or should have been. John still could not believe the miracle that had brought his father to him and was never far from him; Jeptha found in Jack Pomeroy a wonderful fishing companion and was overjoyed when together they made quite a fisherman of John. Yet the spectre of the approaching separation loomed ahead of the boys, grim and hopeless, though each tried to pretend something still might be done about it.

"Maybe you can come back to visit next year," Jeptha suggested optimistically, knowing well that he was wrong.

"Your mother is sure to let you go to Arizona with us for the winter," John insisted, turning a deaf ear to Jeptha's constantly repeated, "But don't you see, I *can't* ask her now with Grandma gone and Aunt Mattie getting married to Caleb? I just *can't,* John!"

So matters stood as the days slipped by and yellow asters blooming among white cosmos turned Auntie Bee's garden into a picture of sun shining through white fog. The boys picked buckets of blueberries and brought them back for Roshani and Aunt Mattie to bake into pies. Becky read school catalogues while her mother made preparations for the big end-of-the-season Grange dinner.

John's father wrote endless letters to his manager in Arizona. He knew he must be getting back soon but was postponing his departure as long as possible, he told himself, on the boys' account. Partly this was true, but there was another reason. Jack Pomeroy knew that leaving Rebecca Brewster was something he dared not think about. She was a dream come true, so lovely, so gentle, so altogether dear. How could he bring himself to leave her? What would life be without her? He shuddered. Yet, would she think him brash to speak the things that were in his mind? He wondered and hesitated, and the summer days moved toward autumn.

What a pity that he could not look into Rebecca's heart! How can I ever let him go! The thought dogged her through the busy days. He is so fine, so dear. Why, I've come to depend on his judgment about everything! His cheery greeting when he comes back with the children from one of their picnics—the gentle chivalry in his manner with Becky, making her unconsciously aware of a gentleman's innate good manners—his sympathetic understanding of the boys—yes, and the warmth of his smile when his eyes look into mine—Oh, . . . Rebecca would put down whatever she was doing and go to stand in the doorway, looking out over the bay, wondering how she was going to face the days ahead.

One evening they drove out to Searsport and were returning by a new and more picturesque route. Jack had been speaking of John's dejection. "He seems happy and chipper as a colt when we're together," he said, "but now and then I catch him off guard and if ever I saw an unhappy boy, there he is. What is wrong? Is he taking the separation from Jeptha so much to heart, do you think?"

Jeptha's mother gazed off into the night and her eyes were troubled. "I am afraid there is your answer. Those two lads might be twins. I've never seen such devotion. Jeptha always has managed to take life pretty much in stride, but the realization that he is going to lose John in another few weeks seems to be something he just cannot face. He worries me as I imagine John does you, and I'm not sure I know how to handle the situation. Possibly a promise to both boys that they can be together again next summer might satisfy them. Still, I really don't know."

"I do." John's father turned to grin boyishly down at her as he slowed the car and for a moment laid his hand on hers. "I think we both know the one way to make not only our two boys happy but each other as well, don't you, honestly, Rebecca? I wish I could think of a better way to tell you all there is in my heart, dear, but knowing you, I'm sure you understand what I'm trying to say. . . ."

And Rebecca with a full heart knew she did indeed understand. A wave of the greatest happiness she had known in years swept over her as she withdrew her hand to clasp his fingers snugly within her own.

"Happy Birthday! Happy Birthday!" shouted Becky and Jeptha from the foot of the stairs.

John in his new plaid shorts and white shirt, came out of his bedroom beaming. He had already received his father's gift, a handsome pair of riding boots and spurs and a sombrero of brown felt soft as a kitten's ear. Just looking at them made Jeptha miserable. John would be wearing them far away in Arizona . . . Maine would be forgotten, might never have been.

His own gift seemed inadequate. It was a handsome knife to replace the one he had seen John whittling with the morning they had met back in May. That seemed years ago now and the knife a very silly gift. He had seen something in the gift shop in Plandome that he thought would have been handsomer. It was a wooden plaque with two hooks on it to hang things on, things like sneakers maybe or shorts. In the top left hand corner was a big red lobster and in the lower right hand one an anchor, and running from the lobster to the anchor were the words, "Don't forget to come back to Maine!" Mother said to go ahead and get it if he thought John would like it, but Becky said it was corny. So he got the knife instead. But he still yearned over the plaque.

Becky had selected some handsome wool hose and Mother a cashmere sweater, and John seemed to be delighted with them all as he refolded tissue paper and slid onto his chair at the breakfast table.

They were just finishing when Auntie Bee caroled from the front door. "Yoo-hoo! Anybody home? Where's my birthday boy? Ah, there you are! Well, happy, happy birthday, darling!" She advanced on the dining room, a vision in sea-green slacks and sweater, her curls bound with a ribbon to match, and slipped into a vacant chair. "No, no coffee, thank you. Most absurd thing has happened and I must be off in a twit. The Mathews and the McPheters got their dates all mixed, so they're *all* coming this morning—seven of them! On the nine o'clock plane at Rockland, and I'm supposed to be there to meet them and it's after eight now!

"Well, here's a little something your Auntie Bee thought you might enjoy out West when you want to keep us posted on what you're doing." She gave John a trim, square, little package which, when he opened it, disclosed a handsome camera for taking colored pictures. John kissed her and thanked her and then she was off and the others settled back to discuss the birthday picnic on the mountaintop that afternoon.

Jeptha thought his mother never had looked so pretty as she did today. Instead of the slacks she usually wore on picnics she was wearing a new soft blue print and against her dark hair she had tucked a tiny clump of cedar with two late white rosebuds in its center. She looks younger than Becky, he told himself, watching her wrap deviled eggs in waxed paper and tuck John's favorite cocoanut cake into a pastry box.

It was the first day she had left the *Crow's-Nest* in Aunt Mattie's care, but as she explained in today's especially lilting voice, this was a day apart and she would not dream of missing John's birthday picnic. (Becky was playing the piano in a summer camp concert at Rockport, so she was not going. What did you do at a picnic with two "little boys" and two grownups anyway? she had questioned airily.) When Mother took down her guitar she tied a knot of ribbons on it which Jeptha remembered seeing when he was a very little boy but not since. Mother was like a young girl today, and she was really quite old, thirty-five. He guessed she must like picnics more than he had thought.

It was shortly after noon when they started and after two o'clock when they had found just the spot they wanted and spread their feast high on the mountain overlooking the town and the bay beyond. Squirrels scolded them and came down for contributions; a deer stopped, believing itself unseen, and watched until Socks, chasing around in circles, barking at nothing, frightened it off. After lunch they played hand ball and then John begged for the sea chanteys Rebecca had promised them. It was easy to catch the rhythm and the words just somehow fell into place, and they were soon making the mountain top ring with their lusty song. Then came the cowboy songs, a little sad, full of loneliness. Jeptha, though he liked them, still wished they would stop. Presently they did.

The shadows were slipping down the mountain, reminding them all that the summer days were growing shorter, that even the loveliest seasons must end. The summer, the picnic, these were over. John's father carried the baskets back to the car and the boys shook out and folded the blankets. A great lump kept crowding up into Jeptha's throat and he wished he could run far into the woods where no one could possibly hear him, and cry, cry loudly like a baby. Then maybe he would feel better.

He was still swallowing hard, smiling stiffly into space when John's father came back for the blankets. But instead of picking them up from the stump where they were lying, he did a most amazing thing. He took Jeptha's mother's hand, and she was smiling up at him as though she did not in the least think it was strange.

"John," he said, "and you, too, Jeptha, I've reserved the best part of the birthday party for now. I'm giving you two boys to each other—to be brothers. Jeptha's lovely mother and I are going to be married the first week in September. We'll all have each other—we'll be a family. How does that strike you both?"

There was a great silence over the mountain. Through Jeptha's mind the words ran like a toy railroad in and out and around the great sobs of joy that were threatening to choke him. Mother—John's Dad—

John—himself—all one family! There would be Becky, too, and that was all right, and . . . "Oh, Gosh!" burst from him as an ear-to-ear grin threatened to split his round tanned face into two semi-circles of un-alloyed bliss. He longed to put his arms around these three people he loved, but could not bring himself to make the move. So it was John who did it for him.

His hand in Jeptha's, he slid his other arm around Rebecca Brewster's waist to catch his father's coat sleeve on her far side. "There never was such a smash-ing birthday," he said in a small awed voice, "never, never in the world! Now we can all go to Arizona to-gether! Oh, Dad . . . !"

And the two who were responsible for so much happiness could only smile into each other's eyes.

"Isn't it nice to have our sons really approve?" Jack laughed, stooping to sniff the rosebuds in Rebecca's hair.

She laid her fingers for an instant against his cheek and nodded. "Mercy, yes, isn't it? But then," she added with mock seriousness, "consider what exceptional sons we have!"

How quickly, how easily things moved once a man took over, Rebecca marveled in the days that followed. Almost before you could say "Ship ahoy!" a prosperous restaurateur in Portland had bought the *Crow's-Nest;* a moving firm had crated all the cherished old pine and

pewter and hobnail glass and started it on its way west;
Aunt Mattie and Caleb's wedding day was set a month
ahead so Becky could be bridesmaid. And at last came
the day when all vows spoken, all good-byes said, the
Pomeroys and the Brewsters settled themselves and
their mountain of luggage—and Socks—in Auntie Bee's
wedding gift, a handsome big station wagon, and
headed for Arizona. From the curb Auntie Bee blew
kisses and waved and wept a little as seemed only suit-
able, while from the house Kirby screamed, "Ring
down the curtain!"

The car rounded a slight rise of ground and Jack pointed. "There she is, *Blue Feather Ranch*. Welcome home, everybody!"

"Whee, look, horses!" Jeptha was half out of the car and Becky hung on to his belt.

"You'll fall, cowboy. Be careful," she warned. But her own eyes were shining, her heart thudding. This was better than Boston. Just wait until she wrote the Shepherd girls! This looked exactly like places you saw in the movies, and Mr. Pomeroy looked just like a father in the movies, too. Jeptha had begun calling him "Dad" from the moment they had seen him and Mother walking out of the little church in Plandome together, and she knew she would have the courage to soon.

John, less articulate, for days had been stunned by the grandeur all about him, the tremendous spaces that went on and on into nothingness. He never had known such complete happiness. Becky, even Becky, a silly girl, was jolly company when you really knew her— and now she was his sister. Jeptha, his beloved Jeptha, was his brother!

As for Rebecca Brewster Pomeroy, her cheeks like roses, her eyes sparkling, she could only smile up at the man beside her as they approached the big ranch house. "Is this actually real, Jack?" she whispered. "Or have I died and is this heaven?"

"It's certainly heaven for me, dear, now that I have

you here," he answered, patting her hand, "and home and a safe haven for us all."

The spotted ponies, the cowboys, the Indians, they were all there. And one day a cage was unloaded from a truck and Maghra stepped proudly from it. She had her long, sunny, wire-enclosed run, and later on a pony with which she had made friends permitted the cowboy who rode it to hold her on a longe while he galloped over the miles. Sometimes she lay stretched before the open fire, purring, Socks asleep between her paws. So Maghra, too, found peace and happiness.

Auntie Bee telephoned from San Francisco that she loved them but could not possibly spare the time to come to the ranch. Soon she was in Chicago, then New York, and finally back in London.

To Jeptha it was all like a dream from which he hoped he never would waken. In his heart he had known something rather special would happen when the new people came last May, but he admitted he hadn't suspected half how much really would!